Issun Boshi

(ONE-INCH BOY): A JAPANESE FOLKTALE

retold by Nadia Higgins • illustrated by JT Morrow

Distributed by The Child's World®
1980 Lookout Drive • Mankato, MN 56003-1705
800-599-READ • www.childsworld.com

Acknowledgments
The Child's World®: Mary Berendes, Publishing Director
The Design Lab: Kathleen Petelinsek, Design
Red Line Editorial: Editorial direction

Library of Congress Cataloging-in-Publication Data
Higgins, Nadia.
 Issun Boshi (one-inch boy) : a Japanese folktale / by Nadia Higgins ;
illustrated by JT Morrow.
     p. cm.
 Summary: Tiny but capable and adventurous young Issun Boshi goes to
Japan's capital city of Kyoto, where he proves himself a valuable servant to
kind Lord Sanjo and his daughter, Princess Sanjo.
 ISBN 978-1-60973-139-7 (library reinforced : alk. paper)
 [1. Folklore–Japan.] I. Morrow, J. T., ill. II. Title.
 PZ8.1.H5348Iss 2012
 398.20952'01—dc23   2011010905

Printed in the United States of America in Mankato, Minnesota.
July 2011
PA02086

ukashi, mukashi. Come, come, listen to a story. This tale is older than your great, great, great, great, great, great, great, great grandparents. It traveled on voices all the way from Japan.

Did you know there once was a boy, older than you, who was just one inch tall? Issun Boshi stood no taller than your thumb. But, as with many small creatures, he held many great surprises. . . .

Have you ever wished so hard, you thought your heart would crack? Long, long ago, an old man and an old woman wished that hard. They thought they'd die from wishing. And what was it they dreamed of? A child to love.

"Even a tiny one," the woman whispered.

"Even smaller than my pinky finger," said the man.

Ten full moons came and went. The couple's wish came true! The tiniest child you ever saw was born. He stepped into the world from his mother's thumb.

"Issun Boshi," his mother cried joyfully, cradling him in the palm of her hand. "One-Inch Boy."

Time passed. Issun Boshi did not grow larger—at least to the eye. But inside, his mind grew with curiosity. His heart grew with a passion to see the world.

"Father, Mother," Issun Boshi said. "I have a wish."

His wish was to go to Kyoto, Japan's capital city, to see what he could see.

Well, Issun Boshi's parents knew all about wishing. With many blessings (and some worry), they sent him on his way.

"Take this, my son," his mother said. "And this and this." And so Issun Boshi carried with him a sewing needle, a rice bowl, and a chopstick.

"Ho, ho!" Issun Boshi laughed when he soon came upon a rushing river. He climbed into his rice bowl and sped off. He used his chopstick to row.

After a few days, Issun Boshi arrived in Kyoto. What a busy place! *Katta, katta, katta.* Wooden clogs tapped the stone streets. A cart's wheel almost rolled on top of him.

Carefully, carefully, Issun Boshi made his way. At last he came to the largest, most beautiful house in the city.

"The House of Sanjo!" Issun Boshi exclaimed. He had heard many wonderful stories about its kind, brave master, Lord Sanjo.

Issun Boshi waited on the steps by the great door. The sky went from blue to pink to orange. At last—*creeeaaak*—the door opened.

"I am Issun Boshi!" He jumped. He shouted. He waved. "I have come to serve you, Lord Sanjo."

The great man peered into the evening. He looked to the left, then to the right. He turned around.

"Down here!" Issun Boshi yelled.

Paaaan! Lord Sanjo's mouth fell open in surprise. He bent down and picked up the tiny boy.

"My son, you are smaller than my thumb! What can *you* do for *me?*"

Issun Boshi smiled and said,

"Those who see with just their eyes
Issun Boshi will surprise!"

And with that, he drew out his sewing needle. *Swish-swoosh*. He sliced a fly buzzing by the great man's ear.

Issun Boshi soon became a trusted servant in the Sanjo house. Princess Sanjo, especially, relied on him. For only he could paint patterns fine enough on the combs she wore in her hair. Only he could find her smallest earrings when they rolled under her dresser. And it was he who sat upon her shoulder all day long and kept her company.

Winter came. Snow frosted the black tree branches. In spring, cherry blossoms dressed those branches in pink and white ruffles. What a day the princess and Issun Boshi had at the cherry blossom festival!

Walking home, the princess said, "Issun Boshi, tell me a joke." But Issun Boshi did not have time to even open his mouth. A shadow fell across him, and he shivered.

Blocking the sky was an oni. The terrible, man-eating monster grinned at Issun Boshi and the princess.

"Oni, go away." Issun Boshi shouted, waving his needle sword, "or else!"

"Haaaaaaa-ha-ha!" The giant's laughter sent Issun Boshi spinning in the air. "Look at you. You're smaller than a mouse! How could *you* possibly harm *me?*"

Issun Boshi smiled and said,

"Those who see with just their eyes
  Issun Boshi will surprise!"

Then, faster than a fly, Issun Boshi jumped inside the oni's laughing mouth. He slid down the horrible monster's throat. *Glump.* He landed in the oni's sloshy stomach.

Slash, poke, swish, jab! Issun Boshi attacked the giant's stomach with his needle.

"Ooooooooow, aaaaaaah, ooooow-wow-wow," the oni groaned. "Please," he begged. "Please, Issun Boshi, come out!"

Issun Boshi made one more jab. "You've learned your lesson, have you?" he cried out.

"Yes, yes, yeeeeees!" the monster hollered.

Issun Boshi climbed back up the oni's throat. He jumped out of the monster's mouth.

Stomp! Stomp! Stomp! The monster's footsteps shook the earth as he ran away.

"Ho ho!" Issun Boshi laughed. Not only had he beaten the oni. Look what the monster had left behind: *uchide no kozuchi*—his magic hammer! Issun Boshi reached out and touched the silver hammer when . . .

Paaaaan! Now it was Issun Boshi's turn to be surprised. There he stood on the ground. He was face to face not with the princess's shoe but . . . with her face!

Can you guess what happened next? The princess and the handsome warrior were soon married. His parents came from the country to live with them in the Sanjo house. At last, Issun Boshi's outward appearance matched his inner talents. *Medetashi, medetashi.*

Japan

FOLKTALES

Hundreds of years ago, storytellers made up folktales in their heads. Often, the names of these artists have long been lost, as they did not write down their tales. They told them, over and over, around campfires and candlelight, in castles and on cobblestone streets. Long before TV and the Web, kids gathered around storytellers. Wide-eyed, they listened to the stories of talking animals, fairies, giants, and other amazing things.

Folktales are fun, but they aren't just for fun. They teach a lesson, or a moral. A folktale can give an example of how to be, or how not to be. Usually, good guys win and bad guys get what they deserve. The moral of Issun Boshi is that you shouldn't judge someone by how they look. Issun Boshi may have looked unimportant, but he turned out to be very important indeed!

Every part of the world has folktales. Issun Boshi started in Japan. But nobody owns folktales. A folktale is like a gift that everyone shares—and it never gets used up. One person tells it to the next, sometimes changing it just a little. Perhaps a magic hammer changes from bronze to silver. . . .

Eventually, somebody writes it down. Then somebody else translates it, changing it from one language to another. In this way, Issun Boshi was preserved, or saved, for hundreds of years. In this way, it was shared around the world—so you could read about the One-Inch Boy today.

ABOUT THE ILLUSTRATOR

JT Morrow has been an illustrator for over twenty years and has won several awards. He specializes in creating parodies and imitations of the old and modern masters. Mr. Morrow lives just south of San Francisco with his wife and daughter.